Tales of Woe

Tay Reem

Owens
Publishing
House

Owens Publishing House books may be purchased for educational, business, or sales promotional use. For details, please email contact@owenspublishinghouse.com.

Published in 2020 by Owens Publishing House LLC

FIRST U.S. EDITION

ISBN: 978-1-7355466-1-2

DEDICATION

For Temi, as proof that writing helps you heal.
To Chelsey, for always reminding me of how capable I am.
To Keon and Kristian, for always being steadfast friends.
To my little sister and two kooky little brothers, for never ending laughs growing up
and for forming our impenetrable army.

CONTENTS

ACKNOWLEDGMENTS

Thank you to Owens Publishing House for making this book possible.
Thank you to the daring authors and poets who came long before me.
They inspired my voice and ignited my imagination.

Contents in this book includes graphic details not suitable for little children.

Mom

Blood of my blood
Rib of my rib
Unearth the forsaken
Doomed to repeat days gone

- *Generational Curses*

Mother's Day

This was much unexpected. A child? Me?

It won't stop crying.

The nurse places the warm tiny body on my chest. Its face is so red.

"Congratulations, it's a girl." She smiles. Why?

It lays on me wailing. I won't touch it. It might break. At home it's the same thing, cry, cry, cry. Wasn't meant for this.

I call Skip. No answer. I call three more times.

Its screams pierce my dreams, my thoughts. Where are my cigarettes? Probably in my bag where I left them. I smoke them all. Temporary sedation.

Its dry wails ground me again. Maybe it's hungry. How do you mix this thing? The label says 'add water'. I follow the directions. The beeping from the microwave startles me.

I try to give the food to the child. One suck and it screams louder than ever. Why? I'm getting angry. What does it want? I try again, it howls back at me. It's angry too.

The bottle explodes on the wall. No dinner tonight.

Day after day, no change. No Skip. I call the nurse.

"It won't stop screaming."

"Well, did you feed your baby?"

"I tried."

"Did you hold her to try and soothe her?"

The thought makes me nauseous. Bile simmers at the back of my throat, threatening to boil.

"No."

"Well then, maybe you should try that."

"Ok."

"Your first baby is always the most difficult. It is a learning process but I'm sure your maternal instincts will kick in and you'll get the hang of it in no time. It just takes a little practice."

I can tell she is smiling again. I envy her.

"Ok."

Alone with the screams again. Still so much energy in a little body.

Skip finally calls back.

"Where have you been?"

"At work, what's going on?"

"It won't stop crying."

"What won't stop crying?"

"The baby. Your baby."

"That's not my kid."

I can't breathe.

"Not your kid?"

"No, it's not mine."

Each word. They felt like paper cuts.

I could feel my stone face cracking.

"I really don't feel like arguing about this again. Call the real father of your baby."

The dial tone mocks me. I'm not sure how long I've been sitting on my bathroom floor holding the phone, but it feels like days. Maybe it was.

That underwater feeling when sound just can't seem to touch you. Vision is a little blurry but you're not quite blind. And your chest pleads to expand but your nose won't open. Won't let the air in. Muscles feel heavy, like trying to swim through wet concrete. And just when you think you're about to drown, somehow you begin to float. Your head breaks the surface and it all comes rushing back.

The screams greet me like a bat greets a baseball.

"That damn baby." I'm not sure who is speaking.

"THAT DAMN BABY!" Somehow, it's not enough. The cracks in my stone face have fallen away entirely. I'm not sure who this face belongs to.

Its room is just as dark as its first night here. Its face, just as red.

"Your father says you don't belong to him. We both know this isn't true but boys will be boys, right? All fun, no responsibility."

The wailing continues.

"Now the new question is, what am I going to do with you, little one?"

It pauses to catch its breath then responds with more screams. A cynical laugh escapes my lips. I drop to my hands and knees in front of the pathetic crib, hysterical.

"Not my kid!" I laugh harder. Its screams outshine my cackles.

"Shut up you stupid baby. Shut up, shut up, SHUT UP!"

My face looms over hers.

"I hate you, you bitch from hell! This is all your fault! He's gone because of you!"

Even in the darkness, I can see thick veins pounding just beneath the thin skin. Its eyes seem to have hollowed in the many nights without food. Good. Suffer like I suffer. Still, its howls have never wavered. Not once.

"Why won't you be quiet?"

My fist connects with its little red face. Stunned, it stops briefly only to continue again, more desperate than ever. So I hit it again. And again. And again. It's not enough.

I climb into the shaky crib. Its body feels even more fragile than the first day.

I take hold of its baby ankles and slam the body into the crib's wooden bars. Over and over and over. So easy, like tossing a rag doll.

It explodes, decorating the bars in crimson. I can feel the warm liquid trickling down my face, moistening my lips.

Finally. Silence.

It lets out one last pathetic squeal. I slam it again.

My fingers are sticky, like when you eat greasy food with your hands but only use a napkin to wipe it clean. The grease never really comes off.

I climb out of its crib and light another cigarette from a fresh pack.

I sit the phone next to me.

Just in case Skip decides to call back.

The Mold

There is a tiny house
It sits all the way
at the very end
of a still stream

In that house
all the way at the bottom
is an old shoe

Inside the old shoe
all the way in the tippy toes
is a tiny mold

You knew about the mold
living inside the old shoe
But you live at the very top
of the tiny house

No, no need to bother
about the tiny mold
in the tippy toes
of an old shoe
all the way at the bottom
of the tiny house

The mold begins to fester
Yes, fine
Fester it shall

You and your darling
throw lots of festive get togethers
in this tiny house
all the way at the end
of a still stream

You hardly noticed
when the mold
ate the old shoe!
How marvelous!

Soon, there will be more of you
in that tiny house
And more still!

The mold too has grown!
Hand in hand with you

It ate the bottom
of the house
Would you look at that!
Hungry mold
Have you ever heard of such a thing?

You see it now, don't you?
It's impossible to miss
There are even more
of you still
living in that tiny house

That tiny house
at the very end
of a still stream
with an old shoe
all the way at the bottom
and the mold
spreading

This mold is very clever
It outlines your face
It outlines mine

And theirs, and theirs

Our tiny house
is a decaying tree
The still stream,
a steamy swamp

But you knew about the mold
and let it fester anyway
Now we are all infected
It didn't kill us
But it should have

As we disperse
and settle into the world
who will we infect
next?

Beginning & The End

It's been seven years
and I still haven't said no
With every step
my heart
feels elsewhere

You didn't even ask me
You just assumed
Guilt weighed me down
I wanted more, wanted better
But I wanted forever most of all

A home where my belly
would grow big every summer
Every corridor echoes
with high pitched laughter
Hand holding
while blessing our supper

My entire being
cried out for it
I let all else
slip by the wayside
to slowly fester

I stood in a corner
and stabbed myself blind
If I can't see it
then it isn't there

I laid down and drifted to sleep

A whisper stirred my slumber
As I woke,

my world of grey
turned bold
I began to float

I left my body behind
Floated above the town
The sweet voice guided me
It placed me
at the base of a mountain

I climbed to the mountain top
and there she was
The whisper turned real
sitting on a lush bed
of colorful scented flowers

Her dark hair
fell around her shoulders
in ripples
The tail end tickled her navel
as the breeze blew

Her silky brown skin matched mine,
illuminated in the moonlight
And when she smiled
the tips of her eyes folded
like feathers

She gestured for me
to sit facing her
I asked her who she was
"I came before you"
was all she said in return

I went to ask more,
but she stopped me short

"There is still time," she said
"I know of your qualms, girl
There is no rush
He is not for you
You will find another
Fall into the world
Get lost and get found again
Else shame and curses will befall you
and your kin"

How dare she?
I answered
"You speak of shame
but here you are asking me
to dishonor a commitment
How will it look?
After so many years,
how will it look to leave
on a whim?
Is such an act
that of a woman with honor?"

Her eyes pierced mine
"You dishonor yourself
by hiding the marks
under your eye
It will never stop
Run girl, it is not too late
I see your doubt, girl
Listen to it
Run"

I had to make her understand
There was nowhere
to run to
I told her

"Everyone I know has been chosen
They are away from home
and I want that life too"

Her shoulders fell a bit
"At what cost?" she asked

"At any cost"
I answered
"He isn't the worst
And after so much time
it wouldn't be nice
to just leave, despite any doubt
He is true
and I can help him
grow into the man I want
He is moldable!
He worships the ground
I walk on
His family are decent people
They love me too!
He isn't much,
I'll admit
But he'll do"

She seemed weary still
"Are you sure?" She asked
"You are a bright star
So much for you is waiting
So much for you to explore
You are not yet suffering
What is your hurry?
You are already on your way
Money, leisure, peace
It all lays at your feet
Are you so naïve?

Right there, look!
It's yours to take
If you pick him
you may never have them again"

She still didn't understand
How could she not see?
I placed a hand
over my growing belly
"His first born has been conceived,"
I told her
"It is too late for second thoughts
We are to wed
And I am to be both mother and wife
The marks on my body
will heal
The child will
breathe life
and I will finally have
a family of my choosing
Problems are for us to endure
I cannot bring a child
into this world
without a promise to be made wife
That is the true
dishonorable act here"

She sat for a while
staring at me
"At any cost you say?"
I sat firmly
"At any cost!"

"As you wish, my dear"

She snapped her fingers

My being slammed back
into my body
right in time

It was my turn
Through my veil,
I searched his eye
Hopeful and eager, they seemed

I answered the preacher
Three cheers for the new couple
and their lovely daughter
That's us!
A brand new family
of my choosing
What have I done
to be so deserving?
I'd quickly forgotten the woman
at the top of the mountain

I tried later that night
to meet my husband's eye again
I found him reluctant
Oh, my husband! My husband
my husband, my husband!
I can't believe I'm so lucky
to have one
My dear husband
I'll shield the world
from discovering your flaws
You and I together

The stars in my eyes
did not match his
That's fine, men are different

His gazes…
Something about them
No matter!

He pressed his lips
against mine
to kiss me goodnight

As we lay in bed
sound asleep
this first night
and every night since
Herein lies
the beginning
and the end.

I Need You, Now

Sometimes
I think I've made you up
Tiny thing
Your entire hand
wrapped around my finger
As we both lay
with our backs to the ground
The ceiling fan
tickling our cheeks

I'm responsible now.
Responsible for another life.

Another life!
A life I had every intention
to love
to teach
to set free

I didn't know
that I would grow
to become bitter

I didn't know
that you would grow
to hate the sound
of my keys
jiggling at the door

I didn't know
that I would soon
spew hate
from my heart,
direct it at your soul,

crumble your entire being

I didn't know
that I would soon
look at you, my baby
through eyes
filled with palpable distaste
With stinging frustration
clouded with horror

I'd raise my hand
to you
Force you to learn
how to hide yourself
better and better
each time you
were caught

Feel your spirit
drift from mine
as I realize
what I've done
As I try
to win you back

As you present yourself
to the world
A force
brilliant and meek
I stand back

As you unravel
the dark truths
of this world
Its delicious shell
Its sickly center

I stand back

As you imagine
the rest of your life
with every man
who gives you
even the slightest glance
I stand back

You build a beautiful life
and then destroy it
over and over
and you don't know why

You eat
the fruit of your labor
But regurgitate
at the sweet taste
and you don't know why

With every accomplishment
the other shoe
must fall
Every victory
is just preparation for another war

I stand back

I watch
I reach out my hand
You slap it away
I try again
I need you, now

The anger
and hate

and frustration
was never meant for you
You were simply
in the way

It's your turn now
to get back at me
and you do
until you don't

I reach out again

You look down at me
Eyes thick with callous
A gaze I recognize
telling me
it is too late.

December

Tell me a story
Rest your hand on my belly
Lace your fingers
in my hair
until I fall asleep

I want to go with you
Where you are,
I'm never far behind
They'll never guess
what we laugh about

They'll never know
what I cry about
Slow down, my love
Let me protect you
No one has to know

We buried a body in the walls
of our rickety home
I'll help you paint
We can hang pictures
of our little family

Lift my skirt
Pull me in
On the tips of my toes
as the wind sways our bodies
Unsteady at the cliffs edge

The floorboards creak
on the third step
leading to our room
I hid every loose tooth there

Her quick little feet remind me

No, we only need one plate
Feed me so I can blush
You let me have the last piece
Thank you for performing,
playing it well

Hold my hand in bed
Suffocate me in my dreams
I must like it here
I can't imagine being anywhere else
Your lips feel like sandpaper

Your lips feel like roses
This is the best part,
where you tell me you're sorry
Have you had enough?
Let's get away again

Take me somewhere quiet
Somewhere to look at the stars
We count as many as we can
then giggle like children
Butterflies rise and fall between my ribs

Put your jacket around my shoulders
Walk me home tonight
We can be quiet
while you show me
how much you love me

There's a leak in the sink
Promises made, promises forgotten
I'm tired of repeating myself
I was really quiet today

Then I fixed the sink myself

I left, then came back
No one noticed
The piggybank left shattered
The fridge left empty
I said nothing this time

There's a new car in the driveway
There's a pink slip on our front door
The kids scurry inside
I'll take the couch tonight
My neck aches in the morning

I spilled my drink
all over the kitchen floor
Then I cut my hand on the glass
I wrote my apology in blood
Then I bathed in it

I heard my baby girl
crying in her pillow
I read her words of disdain
I kept walking towards the kitchen
Then went back to my room

Let's go to the park
I'll push you on the swings
Your laughter cures all
Back behind our house,
I changed my mind and refilled that hole with dirt.

They're Always Watching

Shh, let's be quiet now
Careful not to make a peep
Watch for the third step
If you touch it, it'll creek

Scream, shout
Punch, kick
Hold my hand until it's over
They don't know we're watching

You lie and you smile
Ice cream for all!
Your shaky hands frustrate you
when you tie my shoes

I want to go to bed
The scary sounds can't get me there
Drop me off a block from school
I don't want my friends to see your face

Oh, it's my fault now, mom?
I'm sorry I didn't get a perfect score
in math class
It was too noisy to study

Play it again
The screams and the shouts
The punches and the kicks
Lull me to sleep
I'll be up to speed in no time
How many were there?
When did it all begin?
You're so beautiful when you cry

You're so pathetic when you cry
Holding on to something
long since rotten
How many times?

I suppose we should all start digging
Your weakness would put that hole
to perfect use
How many times?

Today was a good day, I think
It was my first day of school
I didn't want to come home
Today, we put that hole to perfect use.

By My Rickety Rocking Chair

In my solitude
I'm haunted by your memory
In the presence of company
my strength returns

What a fool I've been
A five-star fool, indeed
I do not trust my own ears
All the lies they have heard

Reluctant to open my eyes
All the horrors they've seen
Ran my right hand through the wood chipper
Penance for all the undue harm they've caused

Pictures of your face
plastered throughout the city
'Missing', it says
I know better, don't I?

Not missing at all
Quite comfortable, I'm afraid,
at the bottom of this rickety house
A thick coat of concreate to seal it shut

If only it were enough
to silence the moans
His moans, his moans, that damn moaning!
Through the walls, it seeps

How is one to sleep?
How is one to think?!
No, no this won't do
This won't do at all

A strange nuisance, is it not?
Plagued in your wake
Plagued in your death
O, silence! I beg you

What was my crime?
To love and to be loved?
How am I deserving?
If only I didn't have ears

Well, that's it! Isn't it?
I'll do away with them
Put that old rusty saw to good use
and chopped them right off

With my hands soaked and sticky
I relish in the quiet
The sweet sound of nothing
Oh, how weary I am

These heavy lids are no match
for unwanted dreams
Oh, how I wish I did not have eyes
The needle by my bedside will see to that

I feel no peace still!
Why won't you leave me be?
The need to be more than I am
To dare to be free

A breeze from the window
calls to me, bends me to its will
I surrender myself entirely

What it means to fly, I'll soon discern.

Dirty Laundry

My mother told a joke today
And I laughed
The kind of laugh
that makes you wonder
the last time you've laughed so hard

She seems lighter somehow
Like she's been reborn
Like she's let go

The last time she mentioned him
she wanted him back
after we'd barely escaped
"Just to have a husband," she said
So pathetic, a sorry song

She'd since changed her tune
She told me she loved me today
Said she was proud of me
Said everything I wanted to hear
back when I was fourteen

Back when it mattered
Back when it would have changed things
I was so sure she was incapable

Is this the real you?
The woman who texts
just to say hello?
Who ends each call
with love and comfort?

No, no this can't be right
The woman I know

exhausts herself reliving the past
She overwhelms herself
with expectations of the future
Damned are those caught in her wrath

The woman I know
is never satisfied
She makes me too scared to speak
because I might say something
to make her hate me more

You see, the woman I know
knew all my hiding spots
She'd make me read my diary aloud,
both my intimate and furious words
Only after she'd read them first, of course

She'd embarrass me with my own thoughts
Then she'd beat me for them
I did my best to make myself so small
Stay in my room, out of her way
The furthest corner in my closet was my favorite place

I felt so stupid for wanting things
What was the point
when they'd be taken away
for minor transgressions?
No, I don't know this woman at all

The woman I know didn't hug
She seldom liked being touched
She made me angry enough
to want to run away
Hopeless enough
to have nowhere to run to

The books I read
and the stories they told
took my mind elsewhere for a time
I'd get irrationally upset when they'd end
because I'd have to return to the woman I know

She mocked my dream
of wanting to write the same stories
that helped me survive her
I'd cry and I'd plead and I'd beg
The woman I know didn't care

So I laugh now
when she asks after my mental health
I laugh so hard my neighbors hate me
Because the woman I know
believed food, shelter and education was enough

So who are you?
This new singing, smiling, joking woman
Is this a change?
Or has this been you all along?
Trapped under the cloak of abuse in a marriage you chose

I feel cheated
Like I did not have to endure this
To fight to unlearn you
I feel frustrated
with no outlet

I feel robbed
Tricked out of the childhood of a lifetime
So you're telling me
now you want to put on your caring shoes
and act like they've been on all along?

Forgive me for remaining a skeptic
Forgive me for choosing not to be
the fool who believes you
only to be disappointed again
and have to heal from that too

Forgive me for being angry
and short in your presence
while you've been nothing but pleasant
and funny and touchy and soft spoken
I'm waiting for things to go back to normal

Forgive me for seeking refuge
in my room
even though this is my house
and you're the visitor
Old habits die hard

Forgive me for closing the door
and locking it behind you
Because I don't know what to do
with this new woman
Is she friend or foe?

And where the hell was she
when I so desperately
needed her guidance?
When I was so alone?
When I decided to grow up without her?

No, I do not know this woman at all
I wish I did

She seems like the type of woman
I'd be proud to call my mom.

Beware! The Tower of Doom

Once upon a time,
there was a beautiful Bronzed Maiden
trapped in a tiny room
at the bottom of the tallest tower

Everyone in all the lands
marveled at its beauty
The tower could be seen for miles and miles

The Bronzed Maiden
had the sweetest voice,
but only those who came close
to the tower could hear it

"Where is my son?" She sang
"The weight of my sorrow
is too heavy to bear
My arms have grown so weak
holding steady all the burdens
you refuse to share

What is right is always right
'tis true indeed
So why won't you fight
when I'm in need?
Why must I beg,
scream and shout
before you hear me?
Some water, please?
Some food
and a few good clothes, too
Some medicine for my weary hands
Just a little will do

Will not one of you
answer my call?
Does my pain and my suffering
not matter at all?

Beware of the day
I decide to stop my song
That will be the first day
of doom for you all"

The Bronzed Maiden
hung her head to rest
The ground shook,
tumbled and roared

Pieces of that beautiful tower
began to crumble
Once vibrant flowers
attached to vines crawling up and
interlaced with the structure
began to burn

The wells grew dry
The sky turned black
The cities began to ruin

After a moment
the Bronzed Maiden's song
began again

All was still
The land bore fruit
once more.

The Full Moon Outside My Window

When you're talking in your sleep
your secrets keep me awake
So I listen

It's nothing I don't already know
The other women
you've promised the world to
the same way you promised me

How little you think of me
for remaining by your side

How good you feel
when you back me into a corner
and strike me with all your might
forcing me to stay home

Healing and concealing

How you keep me from my friends,
accuse me of things
so out of character
it makes me wish it were true
Then perhaps I'd be deserving

I've heard it all

Watching you sleep,
you almost look like
the good guy I thought you were
If you woke up right now
and told me I am your world
I'd almost believe you

But the lump growing
and pounding
behind my head
jolts me back to reality

No, this is no longer a fantasy

I think the moon gave me courage
It was big tonight,
filling up the entire window
Something so far away
taking up my whole world

I rose from bed
slowly and carefully
The slip from my night gown
almost startling me

I looked at my closet
then abandoned it

I peeked into each of their rooms
How peacefully they slept
amidst the chaos
I felt sorry for them
Then I abandoned them too

My warm feet
touched the frozen pavement
for the first time
With the moon guiding me
I walked and walked and walked

And I never looked back again.

Dad

Beauty turned to rust at his warm touch
The deceiver draped in white
Slip of silk on his breath
Entrance me

                    -    *Love Potion*

Sweet Pears

Do you remember?
I was so little
I'd watch you
grab a cold pear
from the refrigerator
You'd sit in your
designated chair
in the dining room

Don't you remember, Dad?
I'd stare and stare and stare
You'd pretend
not to see me
as you cut the pear
into little pieces

Then you'd look up
and find me
boring a hole in your chest
You'd wave me over
My tiny legs
couldn't move any faster

You'd give me
every last piece
while I sat on your lap

I can't seem to forget

You always chose
the sweetest pears
cut so perfectly
for my tiny hands
We smile

and giggle
never really saying much.

My Turn

As you sit on top
looking down at the rest of us
Let go of my hand
Do you think it's easy?
Being with you?
I've never had
what you have
When you saunter
they all stop to see
You never even have to try
Forgive me
for wanting to
pocket a bit of your shine
Your dress
casts a long shadow
It's cold in the background
I'm freezing
Your touch
feels like talons
grazing my skin
daring me
to make a sudden move

You're being selfish
You wanted power
You knew I was no match
for you
In that, you felt safe
The loser who'd follow you anywhere

A simple quiet life
while I slowly disintegrate
behind you
I'm appreciative

of the pity you toss my way
every once in a while
I didn't create
what wasn't already there
But I am tired
of orchestrating
your background music
This song has reached
its tragic end.

Daddy's Girl

In the pink haze of my dreams
I twirl in wonder and peace
My pretty princess dress
fans at my ankles

Do you like it?
I wore it just for you
Do you think I look nice?
Do you think I'm smart?

It's time for our dance
The kind a father takes his daughter to
My hands are so tiny in yours
They practically disappear

Wait, slow down
My strides aren't as long
Can I put my feet
on top of yours?

When I lay my head
on your chest
I half expected a heartbeat
None came

You move through rooms
like a ghost
Wait for me
I want to go where you go

I'm right at your heels
Won't you wait?
I promise, I promise
you won't even know I'm here

Save me from her
She always blames me
but I swear it's not my fault
You're on my side, aren't you?

Why don't you ever smile
in our family photos?
Aren't you happy?
You seem to be fading

Ahead of you now
Every time I look back
you dissolve just a little more
Please don't go

I tried to reach for you
Reach out and catch you
Your hand turned to smoke
in between my fingers

I screamed for you
I screamed 'till I felt faint
You should have come running
Why didn't you come running?

I'm older now
Yet I still get jealous
of father daughter dances
that we only attend in my dreams

With no one in my corner
I had to grow up too fast
I remember the day
my innocence was crudely snatched away

It was the day
I saw you
on top of mom
painting her black and blue

My hero
Soaked in savagery
My hero
Lathered in wrath

I was only ten
You didn't see me
grow up just then
Your back was turned

Who's the good guy?
Who's the bad guy?
Nothing makes sense at all!
Where in this world am I safe?

Limping through life
like the undead
Randomly overcome with anger
at the most inconvenient times

I wish I knew
where it comes from
If I think about it too much
I'll need a few days to recover

From time to time
I imagine falling in love
Fireworks, pink roses and diamonds
All I could ever want

The happiest day of my life

Draped in white
Dimmed by the glaring revelation
I'll be alone walking down that aisle.

Silence is an Answer

I often wince at memories
never far from my mind
Memories from young
calling for you
to come play pretend with me
Memories from young
yearning for you
to say you are proud of me
Memories from young
begging you
to put your arms around me,
to guide me

Dad,
Why don't you want me?

A Love Story

I'm inclined to believe
I was always searching for you
When we were young
When love was pure, was true

The good in your eyes
The curl in your hair
Freely, I met my demise
Armed with charm, you didn't play fair

Anything you want, my love
You needn't to ask
Just wish it, yes wish it
Little reason to look beyond my mask

I spent all we had
on something stupid again
Thanks for forgiving me
I'm sorry it caused you pain

I helped you get up
on that throne you sit on
I prepped you for display
My big brothers agree, you're the one

"A miracle!" they exclaimed
"For once, he's finally got it right"
A love so far beyond me
Holding on to it took all my might

Where do you think you're going?
Don't you dare try to wriggle free
I can feel your spirit shifting, love
I can sense your uncertainty

This cannot happen, no
This cannot be
You will not leave me now, my love
I need a plan, a guarantee

Something to make you stay for sure
But what? What could save me?
I schemed day and night
Yes, I've got it! A baby

We wed soon after
A memory my mind seems to have lost
You seem genuinely happy
Good, it'll soon be time to take my mask off

My prize, my prize
They all mistook me for a fool
Always a dollar short in their eyes
The one thing I did right was catching you

With your fancy brain
and your fancy dress
It's time for you to descend
from that pedestal in which you rest

Yes, I spent our last on a stupid car
No, I did not pay the rent
Why are you so upset?
It's a little too late for regrets

Welcome to our new home
You bought it, you fix it
Stop bothering me about that sink
in the kitchen

Caught you trying to sneak off last night
I bet you thought I wouldn't notice
That awful scared look in your eyes excites me
Teaching you a lesson was just a bonus

Yes, there are other women
So what?
I am more of a man with them
I really don't care if I'm caught

Back and forth
Over and over and over
I see those holes you're digging back there
How dramatic, you'll fall in if you get any closer

You could have had anyone
Yet you picked me to lay
If you try to leave again
I promise, you will pay

You think you're so high and mighty
Allow me to bring you down a notch
You're not going anywhere without my permission
Can't have you seeing anyone else, not on my watch

I don't believe a word you say
We all know you're a liar
The kids will side with me
Since they know you're the loud mouth, the crier

You'll never win, my love
Don't you see?
I've spun this web just for us
You can't escape me

So get comfortable, baby

I'll play along if you do too
Don't try no funny stuff
or I'll simply just kill you.

Yeah, Long Gone

Packed his bags
and drove 95 miles per hour
on his way to nowhere
He broke his mirror
The one that looks in the rearview
An accident he can never recall
Never recall too clearly

They waited
and waited
The embers grew cold
A draft settled in
There were never enough blankets
Not for everyone

The youngest laid
snuggled and warm
The oldest sawed at her toes
The cold had gotten to them

Long gone by now
I'm sure
Long gone indeed
I broke my nose
on something soft

Disease in the brain
help me go insane
She rode her bike backwards
Training wheels firmly attached
What did his eyes look like?
She doesn't remember
It's been so long now
His feet planted firmly

on that ugly red carpet
in the living room
His frame imprinted
into the sofa

Beer in one hand
fury in the other
Packed bags
still driving 95 miles an hour
I wonder if he knows
there is nothing there

He's been gone though
Yeah
Long gone indeed.

The Villain

I watch you sleep too, you know
Watch your eyeballs
beneath their lids
dart left and right

Watch your chest
rise and sink
Hypnotizing me
Begging me to stop it

I wonder what it's like
to wrap my fingers
around that throat and squeeze
Would I be free?

When those lips
turn blue,
will you fight back?
Oh, what a delight

Lucid dreams
where you're running
and I'm chasing you
Hunting you

The thrill
sometimes wakes me up
as I try desperately
to hold on to its wisps

In those dreams
you're never quick enough
Never clever enough
I always catch you

In those dreams
I am king
There's nowhere to go, my love
There's nowhere to hide

I can smell
the desperation on your breath
every time you tell me
how much you love me

In a way, you must know
my love for you
was somewhat of a show
A dance for survival

My winning ticket
I'm almost afraid to say,
you've outgrown your usefulness
I wish you'd disappear

There's no light
beyond these dark corridors
I am the thing
lurking behind every corner

I am the thing
powering every illness
I am the thing
waiting under the bed

I want to poke holes
in your chest
But I'm afraid
I won't be able to stop

Watch your blood
sprint up like a geyser
then slowly reduce to a pool
How warm it must feel

Would you scream?
Beg me to stop?
The thought of you begging *me* for once
I'd very much like to find out

Then stroke your sticky hair afterwards
I love you so much
You alone make me whole
I hope you know that

I wonder where our essence lies
Is it in the brain?
I imagine separating your skull
then consuming its center

It would be so easy
to inherit all of you
Always thinking you're the clever one
No one would ever see me

I lay back on my pillow
pacified at the thought
that there is no way out
You're mine to hoard and discard

I turn over to my side
The moon is big tonight
Nearly taking up the entire window

Wish I could nail it to the wall.

Manifesto

In the dead of night.
In between the frozen leaves
and the mystic moonlight,
laid a body
Lifeless and ridged

Running
but can never reach it
Screaming
without a sound
Time with no purpose

Baby brown eyes
like honey pots in the sun
There's no warmth here
The overwhelming shame
looking into those eyes

There's a valley
between the icy mountains
laced with mines,
robbers and sinful whispers
attracted to elusive vapors

In cold blood.
Faced down, soaking for days
Secrets hidden
under a blade of grass
Just enough to start a fire

Scarlet stained fingertips
resisting to wash clean
Evidence boldly in plain sight
Skin pulled back along the cuticle

Biting in the bitter cold

The righteous beg for forgiveness
The damaged shall inherit the earth
In the etching of a new gravestone.
No lingering sentiments of significance
Chaos in the moments of clarity

Just a trickle of sweat
A dead giveaway
Give in to the ash underneath the temple
Make way for the gathering of the cloth
Sinners be damned

Alone in the thick of trees
Going where the going goes
The Undertaker looming in the shadows
Shattered glass sparkle like diamonds
Perception is reality

The gates swing open
for the good and the terrible
Tears roll down mountains
A new world is in order
Lions beg for mercy

In the house with many rooms.
Belly's full with greed and lies
Lines tapered with each crossing
Working 'till flesh exposes bone
Working towards a bleaker tomorrow

A beginning is an end
An end is a form of a beginning
Heroes in hiding
Falling on their swords

True identities revealed

Safety is a priority
Safety is a luxury
Better to bask in turmoil
In step as a member of a crowd.
There's freedom in anonymity

The push and pull of the moon
to the ocean below
A thick mist hovering above
It's almost peaceful,
being submerged in the madness

Skulls lined up along the windowsill
like ducks in a row
Babies squeal like pigs
Cries silenced by the cold
Demons pull teeth, like ducks in a row

In the prolonged duress of generations past.
All must atone for the sins of their fathers
In the delusion of day.
In the gloom of night.
Sinners be damned.

Father's Day

My hands are too steady despite what I've just done. Gentle even.

Shh. Quiet, now. It's late.

I reach into the stiff earth and drag my fingers through until they rip raw and bloody. I looked into his lifeless eyes with blinding hatred. Or perhaps it was actually envy. I suppose it was always meant to end this way.

I'm not sure exactly when the thought first occurred to me. If I had to guess, it may have been a few months ago, right before my eleventh birthday. It was her bludgeoned eye that set me off – my moms, I mean. It surprised me because I never liked her, but seeing the crack on her face stirred something in me. I had to save her.

They were screaming again, my mom and dad. I wish I knew how my sister and brothers slept through it. I wish I were like them. I couldn't hear anything else. So I focused on it.

I listened to every word, every insult. I memorized them. I wrote them down, and saved it for later. I penned them on my palm, just in case.

It's been every day this week, that I've burrowed in my closet. Small spaces felt like hugs when outside felt like a minefield. I wish it would stop. The screaming.

They usually closed the door when they fought, but I could still hear them. Well, my mom mostly – she was the screamer. My dad had a softer voice. I could only guess what he said by her responses.

"After everything that I have done for you! After all my sacrifices! Who is she?" She asked that a lot.

It was the dead of night. Everything felt louder than normal.

"Do you think you can just do whatever you like? You bastard! Oh, you're going to hit me? Do it! Hit me! I said, hit me! You useless man!" She started to scream again. Except this time she screamed for me. It was my name I heard.

I rushed up the stairs. My mom had her fingers balled up around my dad's collar.

"Take him! Get him out of here!" She was pointing to my baby brother wailing on the floor. Poor kid, I hope he never remembers this.

I went to take him away. I knew I should have kept my head down and scurried off as quickly as possible, but I didn't. I looked up and that's when I saw it. My father landed a devastating blow across my mother's face. The crack of her jaw stunned me. She laid there, on that ugly red carpet. Eerily still.

My father stood over her. I'm sure he said something but I didn't hear it — my head was spinning. There was something new in his eyes. Something I did not recognize. It was in that moment that I saw him transform from the docile man I thought I knew. He'd become something else, something less than human. He'd become...a monster.

I rocked my baby brother to sleep that night. The house was silent, finally. I tiptoed back to my parent's room. They were asleep, together. It was almost as if it didn't happen.

The next few weeks bled on. They were only marked by the gradual healing of my mother's face. My dad apologized. He even got on his knees.

"Please. It won't happen again. I need you. I love you."

I wonder if my mom believed him.

I couldn't get that monster out of my head. It was like I was looking at the world with foggy glasses – blissfully ignorant. Now, the world is crystal clear and nothing makes any sense anymore. I know more now, but I still know nothing at all. I can't stand to be around my friends anymore. Everything they talked about was so stupid and immature. Or maybe I was just jealous of how simple their minds still are. Maybe I just missed my foggy glasses.

Mom was in the backyard, digging and planting, when the phone rang. My dad answered.

"No, she's outside," he said into the receiver. "Oh, is that right?"

I didn't like the way his voice went up at the end.

"I didn't know she was that close with your husband. Don't worry, I'll tell her. Thank you for letting me know." He hung up.
The look in his eyes gave me a start. He moved quickly from the house to the backyard, where my mother sat hunched over. He grabbed a nearby shovel and cracked it over the back of her head. She didn't scream. He straddled her. Then he wrapped his hands around her throat and squeezed.

I wish I were bigger.

"You must think I'm stupid." He squeezed and squeezed until she was nearing the end then he released. Then he started again.

"What did you think was going to happen? You and that man, what did you think was going to happen?" He was enjoying it. Finally, a reason that wasn't his fault.

I wish I were stronger.

The monster was back. No one else saw. I was glued to the window, watching. My siblings still had on their foggy glasses.

He finally let her go. Blood coated her neck from where he hit her with the shovel. She went back to digging.

I wish I were braver.

My mom slapped me at dinner earlier. She said I was talking back when I asked her why I had to do all the chores all the time. I wanted to reopen the scab that had begun to form at the back of her head. Where my dad hit her. Then later, I heard her crying in the shower and I softened.

That night, the stars were the brightest I'd ever seen. They felt close enough to touch. I couldn't sleep. My mom was in danger. She wouldn't help herself, which meant I had to. If I don't, she'll die and it would be all my fault. My dad had changed. Or maybe, he's always been this way. I just couldn't see it until now.

Not too long after, my mom came home with good news.

"I got the promotion!" She was really excited. She picked up my baby brother and twirled him around. "God is good," she said.

My dad was sitting down in his usual spot on the couch, in the same clothes he wore from 2 days ago, holding a beer. He smiled and congratulated her. My mom smiled back. It was a good day.

***

Sleep was finally creeping in, so I went upstairs to bed. I'd just shut my eyes when they flew open again. A loud thump from my parent's room. I didn't want to know. I turned over and smashed my pillow on my ear to muffle the noise.

More screaming followed. This time, I heard my dad.

"You think you can now talk to me anyhow because of a promotion? You think you are better?" My mom's screams drowned out the rest. Another thump followed.

Please stop.

Thump, thump, thump. Piercing screams.

I don't know what to do!

The police don't care, he'll be home by tomorrow and we'd all be dead. Mom said so.

I wanted to run away.

I couldn't stuff my bag fast enough. My siblings would understand, they'd forgive me.

Her bones were breaking, I could hear it. I could feel it. My short legs wouldn't carry me any faster. Please, just a few more steps!

The kitchen was on the way to the front door. I paused a moment. I wanted to be brave. I had to save her, she was helpless.

***

It's still unclear to me how the small knife went from its holster to my hand, and how I went from the kitchen to their bedroom, but I suddenly found myself watching his fists smash her body. Left, then right. Left, then right.

She wasn't going to make it this time.

He didn't see me coming up behind him.

Light on my feet, steady now.

I aimed for his fleshy neck. I just wanted him to stop. I just wanted to sleep. I just wanted my foggy glasses back.

I buried the knife as deeply as I could. He seemed more startled than in pain. He bled a little through the fingers he used to clamp the wound. Then he fell over. I wasn't strong enough. I had to try again, before he realized what I was doing. This time, I threw myself at him and hammered away as hard and as fast as I could.

This was for every time you apologized but didn't mean it. This was for trying to break our family apart. This was for every night you wouldn't let me sleep. This was for every broken promise. This was for making my mom hate me. This was for making me feel unsafe. This was for making me see too early. This was for refusing to be my dad.

I was screaming by the end. Everyone had woken up and came upstairs to watch. They looked at me in a familiar way. They looked at me like I transformed.

"What did you do?" my mom wailed. "What did you do?"

"I did it for you, mom." I bored into her eyes, willing her to understand that I had to do it. She can be safe now. She can finally be proud of me. I did it for us!

"Oh, oh! What have you done?"

"I did it for you!" She wasn't listening. She held his head in her lap and rocked him back and forth.

What about me?

"I'm sorry," my voice caught. "Mom, I'm sorry."

She hummed as she rocked him.

"You stupid girl."

His blood spread to every corner of the room. We sat in it until it grew cold. No one said another word.

Outside, I ripped into the dirt as fast and as steadily as I could. It had to be done. My siblings joined me. Mom joined us. We raked and dragged and scooped. Then together, we pulled the body down the stairs, through the landing and into the hole. The gashes on his face, chest and torso matched the look of the monster he had always been.

We covered him with soft warm dirt. We scooped and patted it flat until the sun rose.

My mom dragged a table over the fresh area. I brought the chairs. She made breakfast and we all helped. Then we sat down and ate with our blood stained fingers. We sat outside with our clothes heavily soaked in scarlet, growing stiff in the rising sun. We say nothing. We eat in peace.

Blood & Chocolate

Up high,
way up high
looking down at the city lights
Tiny pockets of life
waning with no direction
This is how God must feel

The curve in her hip
Her cheek, smooth to touch
The white dust under her nose
Her mouth, full with foam

Spread your arms and legs
on the bed of fog
She unclenched her fists
to reveal tufts of hair
Wet from her bath
Sunken in the void of thought

In the sanctity of church bells,
under the guise of divine protection
Her small hands tremble
as she folds her skirt
Her lashes cast a long shadow
Forced to praise what should be scorned

In the nights stillness
it's the best place to tuck secrets away
Fully clothed in the warmth
Hiding under the myth of balance

Tales of two cities
Tales of woe
Tales of greed

Tales of insignificance

She feels safe in the shadows
An authority is a sign of a bigger threat
It's the last point to complete the circle
Or perhaps it's a ring
Beat a bully with a feather,
watch the bully multiply

There was only one at first
Now there are sprinklers in the graveyard
She lays down, back to the Earth
Eyes to the stars
So many, yet they never get tangled

They closed their knees
and I separated them
Exchanging their souls for mine
Toe the line, step by step
I took those toes soon after
as a souvenir

I burned them with acid
Then I buried them in the past
I go back to visit sometimes,
to lay down and count the stars

This time of year,
the cold can slice you right open
In the rivers current,
still bodies flow effortlessly
as I stand in the middle watching
I am its master

This is how God must feel.

Me

O, Mr. Reaper man
Won't you sing me a song?
The kind I can bob and hum to
All night long

O, Mr. Reaper man
Won't you sing me to sleep?
The kind I can't shake
The kind that's six feet deep

O, Mr. Reaper man
Don't you dare stand me up
I've finally found the courage
I've finally had enough

Dear God, Check Your Voicemail

I'm confused
Please tell me what I've done
How I'm deserving
of such endless torment

I'm innocent in this
You have to know
This was not my choice
This is your fault

Pray, pray, pray
That's all you ever
tell us to do
Is your phone even on?

I've been calling
nonstop for ages
My voice is hoarse
My eyes are dry

I want your head

There was a time
I believed you knew best
Thanked you even
for my dear crumbs

Thanked you for a home
despite who occupied it
Thanked you for parents
despite how they gutted me

Did you know I hate myself?
Of course you do

I play with death in my mind a lot
I'm sure you knew that too

There was a time
I thought you were
the beginning and the end
Now I see

You're a mere comfort
in preparation for
the beginning and the end
You exist to ease

Except
the only time I ever felt your hands
they were not around my shoulders
They were around my throat
Squeezing

That time you allowed
the evil into my home
before I even existed
I felt your hands

Then there was that other time
when I begged and I begged and I begged
you to make mom happy
so she could be nice to me

I guess you were off that day

What about all those nights
you kept me up
allowing me to dream and plan
To live in the future
To believe I could make it

To believe success could save me
You allowed me to reach the cusp
Dangled freedom only a hair out of my grasp
Then you set it on fire
I watched it turn to ash
Then fall like black rain

You owe me

Oh and how could I forget!
You let that monster create me
You let his disease settle
You let me get sick
You let me infect everything I touch
You let him slaughter everyone

I hope you know
he peeled back her skin
Exposed her raw flesh
for everyone to point and stare
Then, bit by bit
he chewed and swallowed
until little was left

He made us watch
Did you know that?
Well, of course you did
You were there!

I screamed, you know
I screamed for you

I tried to tell you
they were hurting me
I cried to you
Make them stop!

I felt your hands then
The tightest squeeze of them all

But they were the bad guys
I'm innocent!
I did not ask for any of this
I was trapped
Get them, get them
Save me!

Yet, the more I called
The tighter the squeeze
As if I were the one
who needed to be punished
They were supposed to
care for me
They were wrong
What did I do?

I hope you know
I won't be calling anymore
Right, of course you do
You know everything.

I Wanted My Baby

I see him
He not me
I mend him
He bends me
I love him
He wants me
I ask him
He shuns me
I beg him
He drags me

They rip me

I leave him
He stalks me
I block him
He finds me
I heal me
He needs me

It's too late.

I Have a Secret

She was a tough woman,
my mother
Eyes like stones
heavy and cold

She had scars on her back
Long and raised to the touch
from my father
She gave him matching ones
Tit for tat

She made me sing
for my supper
Wail, in fact
Nothing good was free
Everything was contingent

I have a secret

As the day grew older
without your presence,
laughter from me
and the little ones
who came after me,
would rise to the tippy top
of that old rickety house
Our shoulders would fall
Our souls would lighten
and I'd close my eyes
Squeeze them shut
and wish, and wish

That you died

and never came home.

Forbidden Love

Innocence of a crush
Dangerous implications of a touch
Poisonous nectar from a dying rose
How sweet it is
How unsatisfying
With every taste
death draws nearer

The crow encircles tighter
awaiting the last breath
My soul mourns
It won't last
The end is coming
How sweet it is.

One Step Forward, Three Steps Back

I fell again
Deeper this time
Hazy nights,
drowsy days
make it difficult to pinpoint
exactly how
I found myself down here

Alone in this narrow hole
I reach out
Take hold of the closest, sturdiest thing
Take my first pull upward
Towards the surface
Towards promised peace

As it grew nearer,
thoughts of those I helped
climb up from their hole
scurry across my mind
Where are they
as I climb out of mine?

My fingers slip
I hold on
I keep climbing

Memories from long ago
when my chest would swell
and my throat would burn
and my pillow wet
from obsessing over why
I never seemed to be good enough

My fingers slip again

I hold on
I keep climbing

There was a time
up at the surface
where efforts turned into accomplishment
Accomplishment turned into resentment
Resentment turned into rage
And rage turned into destruction

I have fallen again
Even deeper this time.

Antidote

Ring around the rosie

Black dust, heavy rain
I bow my head to shade my eyes
Here we go again
Feel like I've been here before
I can't escape the pain
The pain, the pain, oh the pain
My face is wet
I can't tell which is which
My life is a mess
The knots in my belly make it hard to breathe
I keep going though
the same routine
It's killing me, I know

A pocket full of posies

'Take this and forget'
No
'Take this to replace'
No
'Take this...'
Maybe
Just one time, just this once
Where is my lighter?
I tap my pockets
Pull out a handful of antidotes
Guess I just caught a break
Take one
Take two
Take them all

Ashes. Ashes.

I run out
Constantly tapping my pockets
Dust into grout
Rain into drought
My mouth is dry
The burning in my lungs
Worse than the pain
I keep walking
The dogs in my head
They keep barking
I scream
Anything for some peace

They all fall down

A shadow in the distance
I get closer
It wisps away with the breeze
Naked, I drop to my knees
I weep, and weep, and weep
Fingers deep in the cold dirt
Black seeds scattered on the Earth
Take one
Take two
Take them all
Reality escapes me
Eye lids are heavy
No more pain
No more rain
Face first in the mud
Sliver of light slice the night
I reach
Finally.

Stevie B.

Your smile
I want to know it

Your hands
so capable
as I watch you play
back and forth with your friends

I was on the roof
looking down
watching you win

You always wear your hat
backwards
Smooth your hair back
every now and again

Then you'd smile
Sometimes at me
I never know what to say

Then you're off again
Beautiful boy
And I'm a memory

I want to know that smile
I want to feel those hands

I build up my courage
Your friends are watching
and I'm all alone

You smile again
Wide and inviting

I approach
I ask you to dance

But it's like I disgust you
You push right past me
and back into the crowd
You don't look my way again

My face burns so hot
I've never felt
more exposed

So stupid

I replay it
Of course!

How could anyone so perfect
ever want someone so ruined?

I play it again

A wave of panic
always follows
The type that wrings your lungs
forcing you
to hold your breath
It pulls at the nerves
behind your eyes
forcing you to squeeze them shut
and will the memory to pass

Fighting the urge to shrink,
I don't know
what I should have done
differently that night

besides not being there at all.

Trippin'

I think I've lost my mind
All my failures are frozen in time

A snapshot
filed alphabetically
in a drawer underneath my ribcage

I'm scared to go down there
It's never anything good

So used to feeling so much
Now I feel so little

My skin
has a current pulsing through it
All impurities ricochet

I'm protected now
Nothing can get in
Nothing can get out
Aha! I win now
Now I win
You can't hold me anymore

I've shook free of the weight
around my ankles
I'm floating now
It's your worst nightmare, isn't it?

Cold fingers
to my hot skin
This is my peace
I pull my knees
into my chest

and wrap myself
in the dirt
over and over
until I am clean

It itched
so I scratched it
I scratched and scratched
and scratched it raw
Bloody and raw
so I poked it
Anything to feel anything

I can feel my heart in my head
You feel it too, right?

My teeth are heavy
Please be quiet, please
Damn you, shut up!

Something sticky and sweet
like syrup from that diner
everyone always forgets to remember,
slides down my brow
snakes along my cheek
and parts my lips

Hush now, please
I'm trying to sleep.

Don't Fall for the Sad Girl

Is it me?
Are you sure?
Is it really me
you're looking for?

There is a bomb
It's strapped to my chest
I reset it
every ten seconds

How many times
is too many times?
Is this a safe place?
Can I show you my mind?

We've met before, you know
You may not remember
It was a little while ago
The very middle of September

Over and over and over
The hands of fate continue to churn
You begged to know me
One day you'll learn

Are you sure it's me?
Am I the one you want?
The bomb strapped to my chest
Any moment, it could go off

Show me yours first
Play me a love song
Help me forget
the ticking in my chest

I'm scared
Scared you'll run away
once you learn the truth
I'm sorry, I'm no fun today

What happened to the goofy girl?
The one you're so madly in love with
Flawless as a glassy pearl
The one you're hoping to evolve with

She was just a shell, you see
A cover for what's really underneath

I'm sorry I'm sad today
I know I'm starting to say that a lot
Just give me a day or two
I'll be back to the girl you want

I don't know what's wrong today,
okay? I'm just down, I can't explain it
Stop yelling at me, my strength is gone
Give me a second to regain it

Please don't push me to talk
Please don't push me to smile
You're going to make me angry
You're going to make me vile

Is this what you want?
Relentlessly pushing for my story
Well here I am!
A pitiful, lonely, frustrated girl in all her glory

Where do you think you're going?
You're not so grand either
Is a life with me worth forgoing?

I expected you to just be there

How dare you make me feel so small?
I'm sorry I've been in bed all day
I'm sorry I keep missing your call
Leave if you want, I won't stand in your way

Wait, wait don't go
Not yet, please stay
I'll keep my demons at bay from now on
I'm sorry for the mess I made

Please come back
I can be that girl from the beginning
The girl you so easily fell for
The one who's always grinning

Please don't go
I've got it under control
Please

This is your fault
You were warned from the start
Why did you keep pushing?
Your disapproval broke my heart

Let's go back
Back in time
I'll help you forget
I'll be better this time

Hey lover boy
staring from across the way
Close at my heels
Promise me you'll stay

Hum by my ear
Something soft
Something sweet

You say it's me you want
I've heard that before
Are you sure?
Is it really me
you're looking for?

The Sun's in My Pocket

Handprints in the sand
stretch for miles and miles
I think we've met before
You seem different somehow

One of the few days
We let the top down
cruising through the windy streets
Smiling at nothing

The fog has lifted a bit
I can see better now
Drop me off by the water
I want to feel the waves

Lay with me, chin up
Naked rears planted
The sun high up, right on top
Soothing our heavy minds

I pretend sometimes
it can fit in the palm of my hand
How easy would that be?
Help me catch my childhood balloon

Crash and pull
Crash and pull
Over and over
The waves never tire

The sun left,
as good things often do
I'm illuminated in silver
A deceiving silhouette

I want to float
Set sail with the first gust of wind
Then drift along after a time
Plugging the tiny hole with my finger

I want to sway
Both feet in cold mud
As rhythmic stories
take me around the world

I want to make you laugh
A thief, I bottle your temporary happy,
pretending it belongs to me
Only opening when there's no hope

Show me how you did that
I want to be like you
It looks so easy
You look so safe

Dance with me, will you?
I want to mimic your moves
Does my smile look like yours?
Can you tell the difference?

If I scream silently
would you still hear me?
Let's will the sun back
You're even more familiar still

Chase me down the block
Catch our breath, hands resting on our knees
Same hands stamp wet cement
We're marking what's ours

Let's run away
Let's keep running
Take what we want
in place of all we've lost

I want to forget
Let the poison sit at the tip of my tongue
If we reach high enough
we can graze the surface

You promise me forever
I promise you a good time
Wires intertwined, tossed into the ocean
Lost forever, cradled by the current

Intimate gatherings
with those who've also cheated death
Pulled back at the brink

Slip me a note under my pillow
The type that ensures sweet dreams
The smell of sweets in the morning
Harmless mischief in our eyes

Follow the plan
The road that will lead to more
It's easier than it looks
Watch me, I've been practicing

We can have it all
Heightened convictions within our souls
Coy smiles and sweet oranges
Naked rears and warm sand

I want it all.

A Few Helpful Resources

National Domestic Violence Hotline 1-800-799-7233
OR
Log onto thehotline.org
OR
Text LOVEIS to 1-866-331-9474

National Suicide Prevention Lifeline 1-800-273-8255
OR
Log onto suicidepreventionlifeline.org

Substance Abuse and Mental Health Services Administration (SAMHSA) 1-800-662-4357
OR
Log onto findtreatment.gov

In an event of an emergency, please dial 911.

You are not alone.

ABOUT THE AUTHOR

Tay Reem was raised in a small town in Maryland. She studied psychology at Morgan State University. After many years working as an analyst, she left the corporate world to pursue her dream of becoming an author instead. She currently resides in Southern California where she is hard at work on her second book.

Made in United States
North Haven, CT
02 January 2022

14015491R00079